STEPPING OUT
THE CONTINUATION...

EVANGELIST DR. THERESA STOKLEY

authorHOUSE®

AuthorHouse™
1663 Liberty Drive
Bloomington, IN 47403
www.authorhouse.com
Phone: 1 (800) 839-8640

Published by AuthorHouse 03/22/2016

ISBN: 978-1-5049-8630-4 (sc)
ISBN: 978-1-5049-8687-8 (e)

Library of Congress Control Number: 2016904695

Print information available on the last page.

Any people depicted in stock imagery provided by Thinkstock are models,
and such images are being used for illustrative purposes only.
Certain stock imagery © Thinkstock.

This book is printed on acid-free paper.

Because of the dynamic nature of the Internet, any web addresses or links contained in
this book may have changed since publication and may no longer be valid. The views
expressed in this work are solely those of the author and do not necessarily reflect the
views of the publisher, and the publisher hereby disclaims any responsibility for them.

CONTENTS

Contents

Acknowledgements

First I thank God for all of His love and guidance through the writing of this book, for His allowing me the testimony to share with others who may find themselves in similar situations and need to know they are not alone. I thank everyone that has been mentioned inside the pages of this book and have been inspired by the message. I thank those that have encouraged me to continue to tell of the Lord's goodness and mercy that He showers on each of us. I thank those that have shown an interest in wanting to know what has continued to happen in my life and want to follow me as I follow Christ. I thank my parents and that is Rev. James Seabron and my mother Ms. Francine Stokley, I thank my children Yolanda and Alexis, I thank Jasmine (granddaughter) whom God so graciously has allowed me to raise and who has been so instrumental in keeping me grounded and I thank the Lord for all of my other grandchildren and for the children mentioned in this book as my other children. I thank each and every one who purchases this book and to everyone that gets a chance to read it. God bless those that are incarcerated and those that have used the first 'Stepping Out' as a self-help tool and may you find the same help and inspiration in 'Stepping Out The Continuation....' From my heart to yours, love, love and love a thousand times over.

Evangelist Dr. Theresa Stokley
God's Servant

INSPIRATION

Praise the Lord, my last novel invited you to join me in "Stepping Out", into a new life, that life is a life with Jesus. I'm encouraging you as I've learned over the years, the trials that come upon you in this life will sometimes make you ask **_"Where is God"_,** surely He see what's going on in my life. Take it from me, He does know, He cares, and He wants you to know that He's working it out for you. So always remember, no matter what it "looks, sounds, or seems like" He's yet in charge. Now please join me as I continue my journey............

PROLOGUE

My last book "Stepping Out", shared with you my life before Christ, it told of my childhood, the lack of love, family support, and dysfunction, it spoke of a lot of the same negative forces and evil spirits that our youths and young adults are yet under attack from. My walk with Christ begun 26 years ago and it wasn't easy then and it's not getting any easier, it's time that we as saints of the Living God began to stand up and take back our children and young adults from the hands of the enemy, we as the children of God seem to have forgotten the power we possess in the Name of the Risen Savior, Jesus Christ. I won't try and make light of what we as the saints of God are up against, this is a constant battle. I know you're saying the battle belongs to the Lord and that's true but we also must fight because why else would He tell us to suit up in the full armor of the Lord.

Thank God for having an advocate with the Father, who is Jesus Christ and He's constantly making intercessions for us to the Father. I thank God for the Holy Ghost, for His leading, guiding and teaching me that no matter what the fight or temptation was or is, as long as I allow Him to have free reign in my life and heart I'll come out victorious.

GOD'S SETTING THE FOUNDATION

Praise God, I'm home now. For those that didn't read the first book "Stepping Out", let me bring you up to speed, but to get the full effect of the message the Lord has commissioned me to put in print, you'll have to get "Stepping Out". I was just getting home from jail after facing 15-90 years, after serving only 3 months and 1 week the Lord had them to release me. The month of my arrest was September, the Lord came inside my heart inside the jail and saved me in October, and in November, He filled me with the Holy Ghost, in December, He had them to send me home, this was in the year 1989. I've been running for my life every since, there have been some hard test and trials and some tribulations, but the Lord has been and yet is *Faithful concerning His Word,(many are the afflictions of the righteous, but the Lord delivereth them out of all their troubles, ps.34:19).* That passage of scripture has blessed and kept me so many times over the years. When I was incarcerated I had asked God to allow me to have a prison ministry, just to go out and let people know within the different institutions that just because they were within a bondage situation in the physical didn't mean that they had to be in bondage in the spirit, mind, heart or soul. I found this to be a truth while I was in bondage in the physical, *(If the Son therefore shall make you free; you shall be free indeed. Jn.8:36),* I really wanted to share this with others and also to let them know that the situation they found themselves in could be the beginning of a whole new life. This ministry that I was asking God for was not only for those locked away in an institution. The Lord had also revealed to me another level of prison ministry, it was the fact that there were people walking around in the prisons of their own minds. As we go

1

through life we can allow ourselves to become prisoners to so many different things, situations, circumstances, and relationships, we're not even aware a lot of the times that we have allowed this to take place and therefore we find ourselves all tangled up looking for ways out and sometimes not finding any we sink deeper and deeper in a place that we don't want to be in nor can we escape from. Upon coming home, one of the first places I realized that there was a need for this particular ministry was in my own apartment complex and surrounding areas. I asked the Lord how did He want me to go about getting started and He had me to start a bible study with the young people, I didn't have a facility in which to do this and my home certainly wasn't large enough, I prayed and talked to God, and I told Him, "Lord I'm willing, but how do I proceed". He instructed me to go to the property manager, and I did. I discussed with her what I wanted to do and that I didn't have the space in which to do it, and praise God He had already went before me and given me favor with the manager, she told me I could use the community center and she allowed me to use it on the night that I needed it and at the time of evening that I needed it, to this day she and I are still friends. The bible study classes began and the children were so excited and they really began to make changes in their lives, once a week they were there ready to set up the chairs, tables and whatever else was needed of them. I would bring snacks for them after the class as a treat, and from that came another way of being a blessing for them as well as for me and my family. I became the candy lady in the complex, this was something very popular back then, I don't think many people do that now since all of the projects in Atlanta have been torn down, but this was a way to more kids, what I randomly did would be to go outside in the parking lot ever so often and get hands full of candy and different snacks, after sending word through the complex that I was getting ready to have a toss up. Once the kids got there I would toss many hands full of goodies. The kids really enjoyed the "toss ups", and so did I. This move really brought in more children and then the adults began to come, some were interested I'm sure in finding out if "tee" had really changed, remember they knew the old me which was a total flip side from the new me. During this time the candy lady business grew. I began to sell cooked food, such as hamburgers, fries, hot wings, etc, this brought in the drug dealers, prostitutes, drug users, the same group of people that I use to hang out with and was still living in the mist of, only now I had a chance to share something else with them, that a greater high than anything they had ever taken part in and it wouldn't leave them broke, broken, sick or ashamed, this high that I was sharing with them was a high that they could stay on forever and it only got better, and there was no down side to it. I began to minister to them when they would come and buy food and have prayer with them. I remember one young man in particular named Stacey, he would come and buy whatever food he wanted and he would always say "miss Theresa, pray for me and put some of that stuff on my head" (anointed oil) he would always tell whoever was with him when he came by to purchase something "come on man, let Ms. Theresa pray for you", and we would kneel and pray. Not long after this began, the young man was shot and killed, he was only 16, I pray that he had made his peace with God, and given his heart and life to the Lord, if his desire to have prayer and to be anointed, in spite of his peers being around was any indication of this, I dare to say he stood in the judgment in peace, but only the Lord knows. This young man lived a short life and it was full of trouble, it was a short life of drug dealing, fast living, and he was already a father, these were the kind of scenarios that has kept me on my watch. As time moved on I was always trying to think of ways to keep my young people interested in the good and positive things in life, from these thoughts came the idea to start a boys choir, now me I can't sing a lick (so they say) but this is what was formed, my "Boys Choir", I had about 10 or12 young men between the ages of around 10-13, these were young men from my son's circle of friends, they went to church with me and they would allow them to sing during the service, the church took them on outings. A lot of times I would go to bed after watching the young men roll out their sleeping bags, pallets, air mattresses or whatever they had because they were sleeping over with my son. To this day there are some that will pop up at my door to say, "I was just in the neighborhood and I wanted to say hey". They're all grown now with children of their own, some of my "boys" didn't make it to adulthood, but one went on to become a doctor, some went on to become positive roll models with good jobs, some active in their churches, and then some that I'm praying will find their peace and grab a hold of hope in Jesus. You're probably wondering where were the young ladies, they were around and I had my hands in their lives also and we did girls things together and they were my daughters, there's still some around that like the young men still call me mama, I have more children and grandchildren than anyone in the world and that's a compliment, all the while growing up the children would always say they wanted me to be their mama, or my son would come back and tell me this, and their actual mothers didn't feel threatened by this because they knew that I always promoted them as parents. I had a firm hand with these young people, I wanted them to know that life was not a play thing and if you weren't mighty careful then you could so easily be tripped up no matter how smart or sharp you thought you were, I always let them know that I thought I had all the answers and all the brains, but drugs and fast living, and game had caught me in a trap that I wasn't ready for, and but for the **Grace of God**, I would have perished. I've discovered over the years that the greatest lie the devil has convinced people of is *"that he doesn't exist"*, and from the way the world has become it is oblivious that the majority believes the lie. Contrary to some common beliefs, one of the many scriptures to put that lie to rest comes from **Rev. 12:9 And the great dragon was cast out, that old serpent, called the Devil, and Satan, which deceiveth the whole world; he was cast out into the earth, and his angels were cast out with him.** Once the Lord cleaned me up and opened my eyes, I would often think, it took the devil over 2000 years to come out with this drug called cocaine, or crack, and once captured by this drug it didn't discriminate, it didn't matter your social status, economic status, educational background, what side of the tracks you were from, it didn't matter who you knew, how big you were or how bad you thought you were, it didn't matter who your people were or what your race was. Many lives have been destroyed by this drug. There is a lot of work needed out here to give hope and the only answer to the way out. **Matt. 9:36-38 But when he saw the multitudes, he was moved with compassion on them, because they fainted, and were scattered abroad, as sheep having no shepherd. Then saith he unto his disciples, The harvest truly is plenteous, but the labourers are few; Pray ye therefore the Lord of the harvest, that he will send forth labourers into his harvest.**

BUT GOD

I've found out over the years when the enemy comes against me like a flood, the Lord will take care of me; *so shall they fear the name of the lord from the west, and His glory from the rising of the sun. When the enemy shall come in like a flood, the Spirit of the Lord shall lift up a standard against him. Is. 59:19.* It's now been 26 years since my journey began and truly I look back and I'm amazed at how the Lord has brought me, not because I've been so good or that I've done everything right, it's the Love of God that has looked beyond my faults and supplied my needs and have dispatched angels to surround me, the Holy Ghost has been right here to teach me and lead and guide me in all manner of truth. The truth of the matter is this, if it had not been for the Lord having been and yet is on my side, I can tell you of a certainty that my life would truly be a worst mess than it was before the Lord saw fit to bring me out of the destructive life I was living, if I would even still be on this side of grave at all. The enemy has not let up, one thing about it, Satan is on his job 24/7, and I can tell he was on his assignment concerning me every time he was supposed to be there, *"BUT GOD"!!!,* when I say that and think about it the Spirit of God truly rises in me, you see there have been a lot of *"BUT GOD"*, days on this journey. There have been dark days when I thought I wasn't going to make it, (yes you guessed it) **"BUT GOD"**. I'm continuing with my story to share and let someone who may be thinking that if this is all being saved is about, then I don't want any part of it, and I know with the problems of life it would be easy to just throw in the towel, that's what Satan would have you think, remember he's very subtle and deceiving. Don't listen, remember Job, how the enemy took all that he

5

had, and desired to take his life, but the Lord wouldn't allow it, but in the end Job had much more than he started with, what we must remember is that sometimes the Lord will allow things to happen so He can carry us to another level in Him. *James1:2-4 my brethren count it all joy when ye fall into divers' temptations, knowing this, that the trying of your faith worketh patience. But let patience have her perfect work, that you may be perfect and entire wanting nothing.* There have been times when it seemed as if the weight of the world was upon my shoulders, and I sometimes felt like this walk was too hard for me, this was in the beginning, but I've found through the years, there's nothing I can do about anything, and after thinking all those years that I was the most brilliant gamer and con artist there was and if not the best then running a close second, but you know what, I found out I really don't know **Anything!** We must began to think like Paul, concerning that matter for he was a scholar and was considered brilliant but after Jesus made Himself known unto Paul and Paul began to serve Him, his words were; *phil.3:7-8 but what things were gain to me, those I counted loss for Christ. Yea doubtless, and I count all things but loss for the excellency of the knowledge of Christ Jesus my Lord; for whom I have suffered the loss of all things, and do count them but dung that I may win Christ.* That's what we must learn as children of the Living God. When we began to understand and accept that it's ok not to know everything, and that errors are a part of life, and we as mere flesh can't possibly have all the answers. Life is much more meaningful than just merely existing, the Lord has a purpose for our lives, *Rom. 8:28 and we know that all things work together for the good to them that love God, to them who are the called according to His purpose.* In order for anything to be that is, there has to be a process, where we are now is not what the final outcome is going to be its just part of the process. When the Lord began to form the world there was a process that took place to bring about the finished creation. In the beginning, God created the heavens and earth, that was the beginning of the process, and the earth was without form and void, and darkness was upon the face of the deep, and the Spirit of God moved upon the face of the waters, that was the next step in the process, then He spoke and there was light, this was the next step in the process, and as we go on through the Word, we continue to learn of the process, of the creating of the world, and the process of the creation of man and woman and all the animals and all that there is. Now we live in the finish of the beginning. That's the way it is in our lives, the test that come to try us are only part of the process that we go through to get to where the Lord is taking us, that's why the Word let us know these things come to make us stronger, because; (1) we need more strength during our going through than at other times when things are smooth in our lives and there are no bumps or winds and storms. In this life there will be many trials, some which will really make us think we're not going to make it through this one, and we find ourselves wondering why is this happening to me, I'm basically a good person, I feed the hungry, and visit the sick, I check on the elderly, and Lord I try to do all I know to do that is right, why is this happening to me, Lord I love you, I pay my tithes, I really do my very best, I heard said when praises go up blessing come down, and I praise you at all times with a sincere heart, why Lord why? Does this sound familiar to you? This is what the Lord tells us about that; *1Peter 4:12 beloved think it not strange concerning the fiery trial which is to try you, as though some strange thing happened unto you; but rejoice, inasmuch as you are partakers of Christ's sufferings; that, when His Glory shall be revealed, ye may be glad also with exceeding joy.* So we have much to be excited about because we are partakers with the sufferings of our Lord and Savior. Another favorite scripture we should adopt at such times as these are; *1Peter 4:16 yet if any man suffer as a Christian, let him not be ashamed; but let him glorify God on this behalf.* I'd be the last person to tell you that going through is easy, it's not but it's necessary if we're to be effective in leading others to Christ, and also staying on this walk ourselves. So just remember regardless of what, when it seems like every devil in hell is against you and every assignment from hell has been aimed at you and yours, and it seems like God has forgotten your name and address or post office box except for bills and bed news, just think of Job, and all he went through, and how when it seemed all was lost, and even his wife the closest person to him was trying to get him to curse God and move on, in Job's heart, I'm sure Job was thinking of the love and peace and faithfulness of God throughout his life, because in the height of his going through his words were; *Job 1:20-22 Then Job arose, and rent his mantle, and shaved his head, and fell down upon the ground, and worshipped, and said Naked came I out of my mother's womb, and*

naked shall I return thither; the Lord gave and the Lord hath taken away; blessed be the name of the Lord. In all this Job sinned not, nor charged God foolishly. It's sometimes hard for us to realize the moving of God in our lives, so we begin to wonder if we've sinned or fallen short in some way, but Job was saying "I may not understand, but I trust God, and it hasn't been easy, but I know the Lord will make a way". If you continue to read on you will believe with me that which Job had to have felt and, I can hear him saying ***"But God".*** I can hear him and recount my own life and say with Brother Job, ***"But God".*** In the mist of going through and not seeing your way and it seems as if the whole world is against you, when you like Job can say ***"But God"*** then all is well. Let's continue to travel down the road that the Lord has planned for me. Let's continue to "Step Out"

THE FIGHT BETWEEN GOOD AND EVIL

Don't think for one moment that because we've become the redeemed of the Lord, born again fire baptized, and that with a desire to run on, and you know all the other saying we have, don't be fooled and think it's easy sailing for the rest of your life, the _**"True"**_, fight has just begun. You see when we were yet in the world we had a pact with the devil, we were probably his right hand man or woman. If you were like me you did everything the devil wanted you to do and if that wasn't enough you'd ask for more. What takes place is this, when your were on Satan's side you had a pact with him and you were in alliance with him and him with you, well once you broke the contract with him and answered the call from Jesus, then the pact was broken and he takes his disguise off and reveals himself to you as who he really is, and thus the fight begins. There was a incident in my life where there was a fight, I mean literally. After being released form jail not long at the time, let me just tell you what a trickster old slew foot (Satan) is; I was sitting in my apartment one day minding my own business, and here come some friends (trouble), well we were sitting there talking and one began to tell me what this person had said about me while I was in jail, and other things so I got mad, the old me came up, just keeping it real, I was a new babe in Christ, and He was yet working on me and still is to this day. I know some of us can get mighty deep, but just try to follow this scene. I was always one to try and make you own up to what you said about me, or make you eat your words, let me tell you right now the devil knows how to push the right buttons, and the more they talked the angrier I became. Off I go down two doors to this woman's house, and she comes outside and I just go ballistic, well we fight and I notice some of the same young and old people that had witnessed my life style change and heard my story and knew my past, also some had come to my house for prayer, were standing around, on the other side of the parking lot. Someone broke us up and as I began to walk away, she said "I thought you were saved, and I said I am but not today" and one of the young men (Stacy), said Ms. Theresa, you know you're not supposed to act like that. The response I made to the woman concerning my being saved, and the comment that young man made to me has stayed in my mind over the years. Before I could get back to my door, which was only two away I was crying like a baby. I felt about two inches high, there was so much hurt (not physical), but I would have gladly exchanged the pain I felt for physical pain at that time, and the shame was overwhelming.

I felt as if the Lord was just so ashamed of me, and how was I going to tell anyone anything again after going out there acting a fool. Well I made it inside and I went in my bathroom and fell on my knees and I began to cry, and I tell you it's no joke being whipped by God. He worked on me in such a way that when He finished, I got some new clothes I had around there for a little girl and I carried those clothes to that woman and I begged her forgiveness, and then I kneeled down with that woman (her house was filthy), but at the time that didn't matter, nothing did except trying to fix a wrong and making the Lord smile again, so we prayed about a situation she was going through and this was urgent, and I knew only divine intervention would help, so I prayed with everything in me because I really wanted the Lord to do this, and also this would let her know that I really was a child of God, and that I was sincerely sorry for my behavior. Yes, God worked it out, and the lady has passed on now, but to this day I'm thankful that the Lord allowed me to say, "I'm sorry, and this is not the way a child of God is to conduct themselves". The people from the old neighborhood still receive me as the Christian I am. I learned a lot of valuable lessons on that day. One of the first things I thought was that I would be perfect once the Lord took control of my life, and I found that not to be true, I have to die daily to the old man in me and the old way of living and thinking. A lot of babes in Christ, have ran blindly back out into the world for the mere fact that they don't know this is not true, they are told that you shouldn't wear this, and you shouldn't go there, you must wear your hair this way, you must wear this on your head, no women can't preach, no you must be silent in the church, you're a babe and you must be taught before you can hear from the Lord. Some of this is true, but first let the Lord talk to them as you lead them. I find out that the Holy Ghost is the best teacher there is. *Jn. 14:16-17 and I pray the Father, and He shall give you another Comforter, that He may abide with you for ever; Even the Spirit of truth whom the world cannot receive, because it seeth Him not, neither knoweth Him; but ye know Him; for He dwelleth with you, and shall be in you.* We as ambassadors for Christ do have roles in the leading of souls to Christ, but Paul said in *1Cor. 3:7-8 so then neither is he that planteth any thing, neither he that watereth; but God that giveth the increase. Now he that planteth and he that watereth are one; and every man shall receive his own reward according to his own labor.* Our assignments are important but we must remember that the final outcome is in God's hands, whether we see the new beginning or not. That reminds me of an incident when I went to my pastor and told him I didn't want to preach anymore and I wasn't going back to the prisons and minister (The Lord has blessed me to be a servant in the field of prison ministry), he asked me why and I began to tell him that no one seemed as if they wanted to be saved, well we talked and he prayed with me and he truly ministered to me, but still my spirit wasn't at peace. When I got home that night I was sitting on my sofa just wrestling within myself, suddenly the Lord began to speak and I took note of what He was saying, and this is what He said; *"My business is my business, and your business is my business, you don't have any business"* I learned from that experience what Paul meant in *1Cor.3:7-8,* but also the Lord showed me something else, His love and understanding of what I was feeling, and also He showed compassion for what I was going through. After showing me my place in that area, He began to let me see different men and women from the different institutions that I had ministered to in the Name of Jesus, and these ones that I saw at these different times, and each one remembered me but I could only place a few because of the many that I ministered to and the different institutions I visited. They would make me remember who they were or where they were at the time when our paths crossed. Praise God, they had surrendered their hearts and souls to the Lord. The Lord loves us so much, I was letting the devil talk to me and try and make me take back what the Lord had ordained me to do. The Lord and His love and mercy for me is so great that He said through allowing me to see these people was; ***Jer.1:5-8 Before I formed thee in the belly I knew thee; and before thou camest forth out of the womb I sanctified thee and I ordained thee a prophet unto the nations. Then said I Lord God! Behold, I cannot speak: for I am a child. But the Lord said unto me, Say not, I am a child: for thou shalt go to all that I shall send thee, and whatsoever I command thee thou shalt speak. Be not afraid of their faced; for I am with thee to deliverer thee, saith the Lord.*** The love and blessed reassurances of the Lord are just overwhelming. These are just a couple of fights between good and evil that have taken place in my life over the years, as you read on you will certainly see that there have been by far many, many more. Always in this life there will be battles between good and evil. ***Eph. 6:12 says, For we wrestle not against flesh and blood, but against principalities, against powers, against the rulers of the darkness of this world, against spiritual wickedness in high places.*** As the battles are taking place remember; ***Eccl. 9:11 I returned, and saw under the sun, that the race is not to the swift, not the battle to the strong, neither yet bread to the wise, not yet riches to men of understanding, not yet favour to men of skill; but time and chance happeneth to them all.*** As long as there's good and evil, there will be conflicts, not all will be in the natural and that's not to say physical combat, but a conflict of disagreements, but even that's ok if we once again go to the Word concerning this. ***Prov.16:32 He that is slow to anger is better than the mighty, and he that ruleth his spirit than he that taketh a city.*** Then there's another scripture that truly bless in a time of conflict. ***Heb. 12:14-15 Follow peace with all men, and holiness, without no man shall see the Lord. Looking diligently lest any man fail of the grace of God; lest any root of bitterness springing up trouble you, and thereby many be defiled.*** It's so very important that we control our emotions, though human they may be, but we no longer walk in the natural once we become part of the "Royal Priesthood".

PLEADING FOR THE NEW LAND

Once my life had been transformed to the Will of Christ, I began to look around at my living arrangements; you see I was still living in the projects, (let me set the record straight, before I go any further, no I'm not anti-projects, as far as the people go, and no I don't think the worse of the worse dwell there, now that out of the way, lets move on) I wanted something better. My thoughts were, now I'm saved and I should be *moving on up to the east side*, right? Not so! I was praying and telling God how I wanted to move to a better place and His words to me were, first you have to prove yourself here. I had to pray for spiritual revelation to help me understand this, the things in my life that I had not overcome yet, things in my pattern of thinking, and I had not worked enough in my present assignment, nor had I work experience enough in this new level of my life. I had to humble myself and I had to remember where the Lord was delivering me from, and then and only then would He move me to another place. This was the revelation I received. Do you know that God blesses on levels, and your growth depends on your level of blessings, why would you go out and get a BMW and can't afford the tag that allows you to legally drive it? Some of you may not be from Georgia, but we have a high tax that goes with our tag purchases, and the tag for a BMW would be out of this world if you don't have the means in which to comfortably afford it. Well I continued to live in my apartment for a total of three years until the Lord saw fit to move me. I was off and running in my new life, not knowing how it would be but trusting God to lead me, because at the time though willing to obey, but not knowing what it was I had to prove or disprove myself of. From the store I was running from my home the Lord had proven to me how He would and could provide. ***Phil. 4:19 but my God shall supply all your need according to His riches in glory by Christ Jesus.*** I was receiving public assistance, and there came a time when the Lord spoke to me and told me to go and get off the program, well I was so trusting of the Lord that I didn't even question Him. (I yet have that same trust). I went strutting down to the office the very next day and told the lady that I wanted to get off the program, and since the reason I gave her was that I had been married for a few months and I was supposed to report it, she gave me the strangest look, but it got even stranger when I told her the Lord told me to come and withdraw from the program, even though I risked a penalty of some sort, even jail time. This lady was just slack jawed, she said after a moment that she would just state that I had voluntarily withdrew from the program, but that she wouldn't state a reason. I learned so much from this experience; ***Prov. 3:5-6 Trust in the Lord with all thine heart, and lean not unto thine own understanding. In all thy ways acknowledge Him, and He shall direct thy paths.*** From my understanding I just knew I was in trouble, but to this day I can still remember that I had no fear walking in that office, I was trusting in the Lord to be in control of the situation, and He was. Then there's the experience of going from door to door to witness to my neighbors, the same doors I was knocking on now to lead the lost to Christ and to pray with those behind the doors were the same doors I had knocked on in the past or merely walked through, to either get high, sell drugs, or gamble. I was always equipped in the past with whatever I needed to do what I was doing, and now was no different, I was yet equipped. I had on the whole armour of God. ***Eph. 6:11 Put on the whole armour of God that ye may be able to stand against the wiles of the devil.*** This was truly something else, I didn't feel like the old me, as if I had never been a part of the scene that I witnessed over and over as I ministered to and prayed for the people that not long before I was getting high with and gambling with, and drinking, partying, and plenty of other ungodly things. As I shared with the ones that hadn't been in my presence since my new life began, the hand of Jesus in my life and how He not only loved me but loved them also, and if he did it for me, He'd do it for them. I cried many times with the people from my past, my heart went out to them then, as it still does when I may run across one of them. I think about how I was such a wretch undone, I hear people say that but

I was truly there, and I never would have thought in my wildest dreams that I would know Jesus like I do. I continued to do the work of a servant for my Lord as He instructed. ***Acts 1:8 But ye shall receive power, after that the Holy Ghost is come upon you and ye shall be witnesses unto me both in Jerusalem, and in all of Judea, and Samaria, and unto the uttermost part of the earth.*** After being in the apartment for almost two years and waiting on the move of God yet keeping myself occupied, ***Lk. 19:13 And He called His ten servants, and delivered them ten pounds (about 3 months salary) and said unto them occupy till I come.*** Believe me there was a lot of work to keep me busy as I waited patiently on the Lord. During the watch night service, (January1, 1992), my pastor spoke and said that the Lord said we as saints of God could have anything they wanted from Him if we only believe it. I knew the Lord to work miracles because He had already showed Himself to me in so many ways in such a short time, so I was ready with my request. Right then and there I asked God for a house, not just any house but a new house built from the ground. I didn't want one that someone else had lived in, see even then I knew that I didn't serve a cheap God, and also there is nothing impossible to God. I also knew without faith it's impossible to please God, so I was not going to look at my money situation because there was none to count. I found out early to walk by faith and not sight. ***2Cor. 5:6-7 Therefore we are always confident, knowing that, whilst we are at home in the body, we are absent from the Lord; for we walk by faith and not sight.*** Well I went home after that service ended and begin to pack dishes and as I packed I sealed my boxes, and I told God T wanted to be in my new home by the middle of the year, (June). I went about packing and throwing things out and consistently packing, you see I already knew He was going to give me my new home, never doubted it, this is called blind faith. My son's bed and mattress was just raggedy and so I threw that out, I lived in a four level apartment and I had boxes packed up from the top to the bottom, my kitchen was full of stacked boxes. During this time people would come and see all the boxes and I would just say I'm moving in response to their inquiry about all the packed boxes. One day my dad came over, who is also a minister and the conversation went like this;

Dad: baby why do you have all those boxes packed?

Me: *because I'm moving,*

Dad: *where are you moving?*

Me: *I don't know.*

Dad: *when are you moving?*

Me: *I don't know, I just know God is going to give me a new house.*

Dad: *well baby I wouldn't pack up all my things until I know when I'd be moving.*

Me: *well God told me I could have a new house and I just believe He's going to give it to me.*

He really didn't believe me but that was ok, because I knew what the man of God spoke and even more than that I knew what the Holy Ghost had spoke into my spirit. Well June came and went and I was still in the apartment, but I continued to believe God and I didn't unpack my belonging, I never removed any from boxes, and because of how I was responding to my belief and faith in God, I was being called a fanatic, brain washed, confused and other things, and this was being said by people that said they were saints and believers. Sometimes the very people that you walk with will be the very ones to cause you to be discouraged and to lose faith. For this reason it is so important that we gain and maintain a relationship and stay in fellowship with the Lord.

Faith Pays Off

I didn't just pray and believe God for my new home, but I began to put faith to work. I went to a bank and applied for a loan to buy a home, not having acceptable credit nor a job but this is the sort of faith we should have, remember walk by faith and not by sight. I went and looked at different homes, but it had to be "new", so I went to newly built sub divisions, and sometimes different saints went with me and sometimes it was just me, but there was always Jesus encouraging me to go on. I tell you some people moved into some holy houses because I prayed and anointed more houses in this city. I saw this blue house on day and it was brand new, so I did the normal thing, I went and prayed and anointed that and claimed it as I had in the past. One day I called about the blue house and made arrangements to meet with the realtor and pay a deposit, well before I could follow through on this the lady called me and told me that another person had come in and made a deposit before I could and since we were both applying for the house and she came first that they would have to sell her the house. Let me tell you what was going on with the apartment at this time, remember, I had withdrawn from the public assistance program at this time and now it's November, and I've received a letter saying that my rent would be in the hundreds of dollars. I began to talk to Jesus, and I let it be known that I didn't have this kind of money and I have all these bills already that I couldn't pay, so what did He want me to do? His answer to me was; *no one is calling you or knocking on your door about bills, and if I don't do it, it can't be done, so why are you worried?* I thought about what He said to me on that day and I've remembered it every time I couldn't see my way. Keep in mind this was now the eleventh month, and there was only on month left in 1992. I remember a conversation I had with my daughter, she said; momma that lady got your house, and I told her I didn't care that the lady had put her money down, that it was my house because God said so! I promise you it wasn't a week later that the realtor called and told me that the lady had withdrew her deposit and she wanted to check with me and give me a chance to get the house if I still wanted it. Well, Praise God! Of course I wanted it, because it was mine, we know that what God has for you it is for you. It didn't surprise me that I got the house because I never doubted I would; the thing that amazed me was the awesome move of God. To this day His awesomeness has never ceased to amaze me. Well I met with the realtor and the money to move in was less than the rent I had been told would start in December, much lower. Except He did it, it wouldn't have been done. I'm here to tell you I rented a u-haul and got my family and meager belongings and moved into my miracle that no one believed. People tried to say I was brainwashed, others said she done turned into one of them holy rollers, and some just straight out didn't believe me when I told them that the house was a miracle. I think of the times when different ones tried to make me unpack my belonging and quit fooling myself, can you just see what would have happened if I had unpacked and gave in to the enemy. There are times when the Lord will tell us to do certain things and because we listen to other people we miss our blessings, had I listened to anyone but the Lord I would probably have been there a long time. Believe me many tried to make me think I was crazy or chasing a white man's God. I didn't care who else's God He was or is, I just knew and still know that He is my God, The God of my salvation.

JASMINE

Before I go any further, let me introduce you to an awesome blessing that I came home to; the name of the blessing was _"Jasmine"_. This is my first grandchild, who over the years has become my daughter. When I was released from jail, Jasmine was two months old. When my dad would bring my daughter to visit me I could look out into the parking lot and see my stepmom holding the car seat with the baby in it but it was to far away for me to actually see the baby, I knew from the beginning that Jasmine was to be mine. I used to pray that the Lord would give me a child with my husband, I was thinking of giving birth myself but God had other plans. I found out that through a phone call when Jasmine was born that she was blind, I cried and questioned God, but He didn't give me an answer at the time but since then I've gotten an answer, and as we go through this chapter I will share it with you. The Lord put such a love for this child in my heart long before I ever laid eyes on her. I longed to see her, but because of their ages she nor my son were allowed to come inside, I could have put in a special request to see my son, but because of the time it would take for the visit to be approved I figured against it because I knew I would be home by then. I asked the Lord in prayer to let me see my baby (Jasmine), well one night He did just that. In my dream I saw this beautiful baby with this pink sleeper on and the distinct shape of her eyes and I knew when I woke up that I had dreamed of Jasmine. When I got home I promise you as God is my witness that she looked just like in the dream the only thing different was the color of the sleeper, it was yellow. She has been with me every since with the exception of a very short while. Jasmine is such a special jewel in my life.

I've had people to tell me that I put my life on hold to raise Jasmine, but I beg to differ with them, I feel that because of her my life was saved. Sometimes we question what is or search of our purpose, I don't know what every purpose for my life is but I'm sure, raising Jasmine is part of the plan for my life and I'm so very thankful from the very depths of my heart. She is an anointed vessel of the Lord, and she loves Him with everything in her. She's quick to say; *"I may be blind, but I don't let my disability stop me from praising God".* Jasmine has grown into a beautiful young lady, full of fire for the Lord, she travels extensively doing the work of the Lord, not only is she a very anointed gospel singer. She began to sing before the public at the age of 4, in the year 2000, the Lord called her to minister the Gospel. Now she is known as the keyboard preacher. I won't tell you everything about her because she's going to be coming out with her own biography in the future. But I will share this; a lot of people with children that God had created in His own special way, has a tendency to set them to the side or not allow them to express themselves, to this I say; you don't know what God has in store for that child. I told you earlier in this chapter that I would share with you the answer I got as to why Jasmine was born blind. John **9:1-3 and as Jesus passed by, he saw a man which was blind from his birth. And His disciples asked Him, saying, Master, who did sin, this man, or his parents, that he was born blind? Jesus answered,** *neither hath this man sinned, nor his parents but that the works of God should be mad manifest in him.* I will share this with you, when I began to take the steps to enroll Jasmine in public school (head start) she had already been attending a school at a center for the visually impaired since the age of two. Well there was a lot of red tape and during this time I went through so many different emotions, hurt, anger, frustration, intimidation, not knowing the different laws governing the disabled, I was given the run around a lot. People would say without actually saying, if she's blind then there must be something else wrong with her, now mind you no one never openly said these things to me. Through it all I continue to talk to someone who knew all the laws and every door I needed to go through, and everyone I needed to speak to, His name was Jesus, Praise God, just thinking about it I get tears in my eyes, and the love I have for the Lord fills my heart. They wanted to place her with others that had multiple handicaps, and that were mentally challenged, well I wouldn't allow this, there was nothing wrong with her mind, they just didn't want to deal with the situation. Well eventually God erased all the red tape and I'm thankful He did because my patience had about run out. Now Jasmine was finally in public school and the Lord spoke to me and said; ***<u>Now stand back and I'm going to show the world who she is</u>***; and I tell you, not boasting or bragging on her but on what the Lord has and still is doing in and through her, He is doing just what He said He would. I just wanted to take time and share with you one of the greatest miracles God has placed in my life.

Satan is Always Busy

I moved into this new house and everything was just wonderful, but you know Satan wasn't going to let it remain that way. The church I attended was in walking distance of my new house, and the neighbors seemed so friendly. After living there about a year, I still had not signed a contract to buy the house, I didn't have a reason why, I just hadn't. The real estate office began to call and try to make arrangements to buy the house, they mailed out a contract, but I still wouldn't sign. I told them I wasn't ready to make a decision at the time and if they would just let me think about it for a while. During this time it was hard to make ends meet, I had come from paying less than $100.00, a month in rent to a few hundred dollars a month along with other bills, that I didn't have in public housing, and the funds we had just didn't meet the need. I got in touch with the owner of the property and told him my situation and he allowed us to stay in that house for the next eight months without paying another cent. Look at God. One day I was lying down taking a nap and when I woke up it was almost time to go to a evening service and I was contemplating going that evening because I wasn't feeling the best, but the Lord spoke and told me to get up and go on, I got up got dressed and went to the service. Thank God for Jesus, when we got home that night the front door was standing open and the home alarm was going off, someone had broke into the house. To this day I wonder what would have happened if the Lord had not woke me up and told me to go to the service, also as important as His waking me up is the fact of what would have happened if I hadn't obeyed. They took all kinds of things including a microwave that worked as if it was on its way out. By this time I'm beginning to believe that our season here is about over, I'm also beginning to feel as if God is in the mist of my not signing the contract. We didn't move or anything at that time, this was one of two break-ins. We had this car at the time that had begin to give us a lot of trouble and we were still paying for it, and I promise you that it couldn't climb a hill over ten mph, and on top if that it smoked all the way. I got a lot of stares and hand gestures while driving that car, but it was all we had. Just as we got down to the last few payments, it got hard to make the notes, one morning I got up and looked out of the window and the car was gone, (repossessed), now by this time I'm really trying to figure out what is going on, but I know God is yet in charge, my faith was so strong at this time, the true innocence of a small child, depending on and trusting her daddy. *Matt. 19:14 But Jesus said, Suffer little children, and forbid them not, to come unto me; for of such is the kingdom of heaven.* Now we were without a form of transportation and living in a house that not only didn't belong to us, but we were also not paying anything to be there. Within a couple of weeks the Lord blessed us with another car that ran very well and we were only charged a fraction of the cost at very small payments. Sometimes the Lord has to take something away from us so He can bless us with something better and we try to hold on to the junk, you see we were steady putting money into something we would never fully benefit from, so the Lord had to literally have someone come and move it, and when I say He truly replaced it with something so much better, you can believe it because we don't serve a cheap God. Things went along pretty smoothly for a while, now we know Satan is not going to tolerate that very long. Our first Christmas season in the house marked the second break-in. While at church for the Christmas program, and the spirit was very high and I've always become very weepy and emotional at anything that portrays the life of Our Lord. Well we left church that night and got home and the devil had struck again, I had already been talking to the Lord about moving again, but this really tested my faith. This was the end of the first year in the house, the thief had made off with a Sega game my son had under the tree, and some games and other things, and broke a bedroom window. The Lord stepped in Himself again and let me know that He was right there. *Heb. 13:5 Let your conversation be without covetousness; and be content with such things as ye have; for He hath said, I will never leave thee, nor forsake thee.* He is so very faithful. The policemen that came, bless their hearts, took all the information, and then they asked what was taken and I told them, they told me if it was ok they wanted to replace my son's game system and games and they also gave me a new fifty dollar bill to pay to have the window replaced, now I know that was God. The policeman brought that game to my son in time to put it under the tree, and that's not all he got a second game from somewhere else. *Mal. 3:10 Bring ye all the tithes into the storehouse, that there might be meat in mine house, and prove me mow herewith, saith the Lord of hosts, if I will not pour you out a blessing, that there shall not be room enough to receive it.* Being tithe payers the Lord was only being true to His Word, my son had more games than he could use. I pray for the family of the officer that showed so much kindness to me and mine, not long after this incident (maybe a month) he was killed in the line of duty. After the second break-in I truly began to seek the face of God concerning another new house, part of my partition to the Lord went like this; Father I appreciate this shelter that you blesses us to receive at the time when it was needed the most, I don't want to seem ungrateful or unthankful, but I really don't want to continue to live here I don't feel safe at all, and I really don't want to invest any money in this place. For those who don't see where I'm going well, I was proving God (Mal. 3:10), again the Lord began to lead me. By this time the landlord had asked me if I could began to pay rent and if I could, how much I wanted to pay, look at the favor of God. I had lived in this new house for little more than a year and it had truly been a time of test and trials, yet most important of all was the spiritual growth and strength the Lord allowed me. I've thought back over the years and there have been times when the first lessons I learned are as effective now as they were then. Well after talking to the Lord about what was in my heart, and the concerns I had about them. *1Peter 5:7 Casting all your care upon Him; for He careth for you.* Also, there's *Phil 4:6 be careful for nothing; but in every thing by prayer and supplication with thanksgiving let your requests be make known unto God.* Through these scriptures I found that the Lord was just a s concerned as I was, and it was ok to go to Him and not feel ungrateful, so in having the Holy Ghost reveal this to me, I once again began to operate in the faith concerning the matter of housing and not just any house, but once again a new house, not knowing how the Lord was going to do it but knowing that He would, that was enough for me. Now I told you about a microwave that was on the outs almost and I told you about a car that was barley making it up hills. There was a reason why I mentioned these things and I explained how the Lord fixed the situation with the car, how He just came in the mist of it all in such a way and proved Himself to be so faithful. Now as you continue to read on in the chapters to come, you will also come again upon the microwave that was on its last leg, as well as others situations where the great move of God came in and with His mighty acts and strong power, made what the devil meant for my bad and turned it around for my good. I pastor used to say I don't know what it is, but it seems like this sister picks God's pockets, because whatever she ask for He just gives it to her. Well I wasn't picking God's pockets so to speak, but I was grafted into the royal family of God by faith and that was all I knew, how to trust God and lean and depend on Him, for I knew then and still know and believe to this day that He know what's best for me.

FAITH AT WORK

Not knowing which way to go, I would pray for guidance, ***Prov.3:5-6 Trust in the Lord with all thine heart; and lean not into thine own understanding. In all thy ways acknowledge Him, and He shall direct thy paths.*** Every time the Lord would tell me, take a certain step or move in a direction, and then I would move. One of the directions He sent me in was with a program called, Habitat for Humanity, this was in February of 1994. This was a program that allowed low to moderate income singles or couples with children and were really trying but couldn't afford all the down payments and finance charges, and all the loans and other monies involved with the purchase of a home. I had applied for the program about five or six years earlier and was turned down, this crossed my mind but I was putting my faith to work, back when I first applied I didn't belong to the royal family and I wasn't an heir or joint heir with Jesus. ***James 2:17=20 Even so faith, if it hath not works, is dead, being alone. Yea, a man may say, Thou hast faith, and I have works; shew me thy faith without thy works, and I will shew thee my faith by my works. Thou believest that there is one God; thou doest well; the devils also believe, and tremble. But wilt thou know, O vain man, that faith without works is dead?*** I made the phone call and was qualified to receive a application (yes, you had to qualify for an application), there was an issue of credit which was the only thing that would seem to be a problem to someone else but not to me, my husband at the time told me "not to bother those people, because our credit was shot", I mean dead, but this was my response to him "God said I could have another brand new house, and I'm going to have it!" I knew the credit was shot, so I began to pray about that, you see the Lord will let us know some specific things that we need to pray about at different times. After receiving directions from the Holy Ghost, I began to write letters to the businesses that were owed and to make good faith payments at others. I mean it was almost like the Holy Ghost was sitting right beside me as I typed out the letters and He was there whispering in my spirit as I made the phone calls. After all the information was gathered and the letters typed and phone calls made, I mailed in the application and thanked God in advance, as I had from the day He placed the vision in my spirit and began the manifestation of His Holy guidance. Next I went to a state funded program that will also allow you to rent a home if you had low to a modest income, and there was a possibility that you would have no monthly payments, but you couldn't own it. I went through the application process and waited on the full manifestation of the blessing that I knew the Lord was going to bring to pass. Now I had moved in the natural believing the Lord to move in the spirit, see that's faith at work. *Heb. 11:6 but without faith it is impossible to please Him; for he that cometh to God must believe that He is, and that He is a rewarder of them that diligently seek Him.* Well I continued to go about my daily activities, in searching for locations, I began to visualize in my spirit how I would set up my furniture and how pictures would look on the walls. I actually moved in the new home before I ever saw it, or knew where it would be. I had not heard a word from anyone telling me I would be getting a home (no earthly person), but I had already heard from the one that could and would make it happen (my Lord). This was back in February of '94, and in April of that same year, Habitat called and informed me that they would be building us a brand new home, and also I received another phone call from the other agency saying I had qualified for a home through their program, all I had to do was set up an appointment to do the paper work, both phone calls came through on the same day. *Mal.3:10-12 Bring ye all the tithes into the storehouse, that there may be meat in mine house and prove me now herewith, saith the Lord of hosts, if I will not open you the windows of heaven, and pour you out a blessing, that there shall not be room enough to receive it. And I will rebuke the devoured for your sakes, and he shall not destroy the fruits of your ground, and neither shall your vine cast her fruit before the time in the field, saith the Lord of hosts. And all nations*

shall call you blessed; for ye shall be a delightsome land, saith the Lord of hosts. Had I listened to people around me, we wouldn't have had this wonderful blessing from the Lord manifested in our lives. Sometimes we allow people to interfere with our faith and trust in God, and we want to believe they have the best intentions and concerns, but I'm sorry to say this is not always true. Really the point I'm trying to make is this, when the Lord guides in a unique direction, we have to do as Mary the mother of Jesus did the angel appeared to her and told her that she would bare a son, **she pondered those things in her heart.**

The Manifestation
of the Blessing

In August of that year the breaking of ground began as this house was being constructed, and as I watched the hand of God at work and all of this favor He was giving to ones such as us. Rom. 2:11 for there is not respect to persons with God. I truly learned this from personal experience. The foundation of the house was being laid and I listened to the Holy Ghost as He began to teach through experience. I don't know all of the builder's terminologies, but I watched as every section was roped off for each room and I watched as every measurement was checked and rechecked to be sure that everything was precise. The foundation was squared off, everything was done to the letter, and by chance something went wrong or was off a inch or so it was taken apart and redone so that all components would fit together as it should, so that it could support the weight and elements of the weather over the years. That it would stand in the mist of the storms, lightening strikes, (in which there did come a lightening strike to the house, but that will come later as you read on) floods, just the test of times. That's what the Lord Jesus is for us, He is our firm foundation, and we are equipped with the Holy Ghost to endure the storms of life and any obstacle that may come upon us. Sometimes there may be found something in us that is off center at different times and God the Father who is the Master Builder, will take that which needs to be corrected and correct it so all through this natural life there will come times when we will need to have different components of ourselves made over or removed or sometimes its just a spot that needs to be cleaned up. Regardless of what it is the master Builder, know what it is and just how to fix it. In December of that same year we were moving in almost two years to the day we moved in house before this one. What a beautiful home it was, the Lord saw fit for the house to come equipped with all new appliances, wall to wall carpeting, and other things that I knew were only there because of the favour of the Lord. ***Prov. 3:3-4 Let not mercy and truth forsake thee; bind them about thy neck; write them upon the table of thine heart; so shalt thou find favour and good understanding in the sight of God and man.*** I've tried the Lord over and over again, and I find no failure in Him, all we need to do is trust and believe the Lord in all things, for He is faithful. I still sometimes sit and wonder at the marvels that the Lord has performed in me, through me, and for me, all just because of His love for me. We moved into the brand new house built form the ground, one room was dedicated to the Lord. I had promised Him that if He gave me another house I would dedicate a room just to Him, not as a bribe or deal of anything like that, because the whole house belonged to Him, but as a way to say Thank You, and that this is a special place in the house just for you. I couldn't build Him a temple but I could dedicate a special room just for Him. I share this because someone needs to know that it's ok to ask the Lord for our daily needs, and shelter is a need. Jesus taught the disciples to pray ....***and give us this day our daily bread.....Phil.4:19 But my God shall supply all your need according to His riches in glory by Christ Jesus.*** Sometimes the followers of Christ Jesus are lead to believe that it's some sort of sin to ask for material blessings, and therefore are living beneath their privileges. ***3John.1:2 Beloved I wish above all things that thou mayest prosper and be in health, even as thy soul prospereth.*** He never intended for us to go without, but because of lack of knowledge we have been led to believe that we are to be always denying ourselves, not so, that's not the kind of God we serve, as believers we are heirs and joint heirs with Christ. Therefore all that belongs to the Father also belongs to us, put here to meet our daily needs as the Holy Ghost maintains the spirit man, as we follow His directions and instructions.

THE EXTRAS

Well, "Praise God" we're in the house now. Remember earlier I told you about a microwave, here is the story of the microwave that wouldn't hardly work, it had about out lived its days and I really needed another one, but I guess the thieves had no way of knowing that, they only saw something that they probably thought they could sell or maybe use themselves. It couldn't have lasted more than a month or so I'm sure. So now let me tell you about the extras. When we moved in the new home there was a large backyard and some people when they could, would make a path from the street behind my house to get to the street in front of my house. I spoke to the people that sponsored the building of the house and they put a fence around my property, that was the first extra, and then they wanted to know if there was anything else they could do for us, talk about the favor of God, as if they hadn't already done enough. I told them about the microwave and one day a delivery came and yes, you guessed it, a brand new microwave which was the second extra. One day a truck pulled up at my house, this was a gravel truck; the driver came to my door and informed me that he had gravel for my backyard. Now I had no idea what this was all about until he told me that it was to fill a dip at the top of my driveway, which filled with water when it rained. He informed me that the person in charge of the volunteers and sponsors that built my home had placed the order. I allowed him to pour the gravel and afterwards I called the person, and she told me that while she was there once that she had noticed the dip in the ground had filled with water, (it had rained the day she was over). The little sink in the ground wasn't large at all, but again the favor of God. This was extra number three. There's a song that says, **you can't beat God's**

giving no matter how you try, the more you give the more He gives to you. Sometimes we give and give and there never seem to be anything returned, we may find ourselves getting discouraged and feeling like when will we be on the receiving end. We began to question God, Lord where is everyone when I'm in need. God where are you don't you see, don't you care? My advice to you is to just hold on, I've been there myself, even Jesus asked, my God, why has thou forsaken me. God doesn't leave us and He is always concerned about us. We have to get away from the way things appear to be. Picture this with me; you're sitting in a theatre and you're attending a stage play, one scene has just ended and the curtain has closed, and the lights have faded from the stage, now you can't see anything going on, right? You're just sitting waiting for the next scene to start, even though you're not aware what it will be, you can't see the stage hands and what part they're playing, you can't see the people that are working with the lights to see exactly what they are doing, the performers, you can't see how they are preparing for the next scene, what I'm saying is that we can't see anything of what's about to take place but we've paid our money to attend believing it will be something we'll enjoy. Then the curtain open and the lights on stage are bright again, the scene has changed and the performers are in different costumes, the lightening may be different. Now we didn't see any of this taking place but things were happening behind the curtains, and we were pleased when it finally came into view. That's the way it is with God, we may not be able to see what He is doing, but trust me He is working behind the scenes for your good and mine. He has a plan for our lives and has the blueprint for it all. *So when you can't trace Him, learn to yet trust Him. Amen.*

Sending Up Timber

Ok, now we're settled in and the work truly begins. I'm looking forward to this new and exciting life that the Lord has brought me into. I'm still associated with the prisons, state, city and local facilities that I was volunteering with when I was first released, and since I had asked the Lord to allow me to continue with these ministries I sought out the different chaplains in charge so that I could find a spot to go in and carry the "Good News". From the youth facilities to the adult facilities, the Lord has truly been in the mist and blessing. I found so much spiritual fulfillment working with the prison ministry. Many people don't seek this ministry for the simple fact that its not a glorified ministry, no one pats you on the back, and you're not recognized by _man_ as doing an awesome work, and your name is not in lights, but I'm reminded of a passage of scripture in God's word; Matt. *25:33-40 And he shall set the sheep on his right hand, but the goats on the left. Then shall the King say unto them on his right hand, Come, ye blessed of my Father, inherit the kingdom prepared for you from the foundation of the world: For I was an hungered, and ye gave me meat; I was thirsty, and ye gave me drink; I was a stranger, and ye took me in: Naked, and ye clothed me; I was sick, and ye visited me; I was in prison, and ye came unto me. Then shall the righteous answer him saying, Lord, when saw we thee a hungered, and fed thee? Or thirsty, and gave thee drink? When saw we thee a stranger, and took thee in? Or naked, and clothed thee? Or when saw we thee sick, or in prison, and came unto thee? And the King shall answer and say unto them, Verily I say unto you, Inasmuch as ye have done it unto one of the least of these my brethren, ye have done it unto me.* For this reason I thank God for the opportunity to be a part of so great a work. During the years of the ministry I have come across some very heartbreaking stories, and mostly all of them pertained to the lack of love felt or themselves lacking the knowledge of how to show it or receive it when it was offered. I've found that; **_LOVE_**, such a small word, but carries a wealth of so much if we can only capture the essence of what all it Intel.

If we can ever walk in the agape love that Jesus walks in and not this faucet love that we turn on and off when it suits us then we as inhabitants of this world would be the better for it. But through the wounds and what I call battle scars of life we don't trust ourselves to love or be loved and that's because we look for love in all the wrong places for all the wrong reasons, whether its to please another, get our own way, win the acceptance of another, false happiness, mask our true feelings or expectations, if we can look inside ourselves and accept what we see and began to work on it then the love that we so desperately need and are in search of will be revealed to us, and the answer is Jesus Christ, for we know because of His love for us He gladly laid down His life, and I'll even give you something else, God the Father loved us so much that He gave His only son. What mother or father would give their only son or for that matter any son whether they had more than one, for a world of people that didn't love or respect them, and wasn't guilty of anything but trying to help. Back to the prison ministry, again let me just reiterate how rewarding I find the prison ministry to be, on one occasion while leaving a maximum security prison in south Georgia, there was a car full of us, and the Spirit of God was so high inside that car, because at the prison there was such an outpouring of God's anointing that when we left there He (The Holy Ghost) was still with us, so as we drove down the highway headed home, I promise you, there was a mist inside the car with us, and I remember to this day how I felt, I wanted to just get my husband to pull over on the median and everybody just get out and praise God in the dance, well we didn't do that but I guarantee you we gave it to Him in uplifted voices and song, I'll never forget that time, and there have been other times that have just stood out. I was invited to attend a baptismal service at this same prison and when I tell you watching those grown men, and once hardened criminals, breaking out in tears and praises, it just blessed my heart to be a part of such an awesome experience, I thank God for the favor that He has allowed me within the prison walls, I was the only minister in the history of that prison to be asked to run a three night revival and during this revival many of the men came and gave their lives to the Lord, the ministry that God allowed me to oversee had the largest turn out of all the ministries that brought the Gospel to that particular prison, this is not for my glory then nor now, I don't boost in me, all Praise, Honor and Glory, belongs to Almighty God. I've gained so many sons and daughters over the years from going inside the prison walls. I remember when I was inside the jail myself, it was called the devil's stomping grounds, but I'm here to let someone know all things belong to God and all souls belong to Him, its up to the individual who he wants to belong to, there is no place that God can't and won't come and rescue you from. I've always thanked the Lord for allowing me to be a part of such a rewarding part of His vineyard. There are so many areas in which we can work for the Lord, and often times we question God as to what is my purpose, what do you have for me to do, what is my station in life, what was I placed here to do? All of these questions and more we find ourselves asking God, my answer to you is; just go out and just say for instance, if you were walking and someone passed by you in a car, what would you want to happen for you? You would want a ride, right. Well that was just an example, but what I'm saying is we are to be a help to the less fortunate, that's what the Lord would have us to do. You say well this is a new time in which we live, and to that I say true, but how many times do the Lord tell us to go and minister to a certain person's needs, be it in word or deed, and because "we" don't feel like the Lord would be telling us to go to this person, than we won't do it. A lot of times we miss what God has called us to do because we feel like we're bigger or better than the assignment, come off your high horse people and hear the voice of God. My son told me once; momma I don't like for you to go into those prisons because something may happen to you, what if they riot or something? My answer to him was; I don't worry about that because I love what I do and I know that God told me to do it, and if by chance something should happen and I lose my life, then I have a place with God. I meant those words then and I still stand by them today. Life moved on pretty smoothly and I continued to go forth in the ministry, never experiencing some of the rewarding moments I went through as the Lord opened door after door, it wasn't always smooth, remember I said pretty smooth. I went through a test in my body, I was hospitalized during this period in my life, but praise be to God I came out victorious, this was the kind of hospital that you went to if you had money and or good insurance, which I had neither one. My husband came to visit me one day and he jokingly said; Tee what you doing laying up in these people hospital, and I told him; this is my daddy's hospital and what's His is mine, and I can lay here as long as I want to, I mean I had a private room, with no insurance or money, but you know what I did have? *The Favor of God!* I always pray the favor of God in my life because when you pray that God give you money or handle a situation a certain way, I feel that you tie the hands of God because we never know how God has chosen to attend to certain situations in our lives and so we say; Lord give me this amount of money or Lord fix it this way or send it this way and then if the Lord has deemed it to be done another way without money or the way you see fit to have it done, then guess what? Yes, you got it, it won't happen or it will delay the process. That's why it's so important that we ask for the *"Will of God and His Divine Favor"* be done in our lives. I was talking to a friend the other day as we were leaving a teaching and ministry session and I was sharing with her that I was waiting to hear from God with a clarity concerning something I had before Him, and she said why won't God just give us an answer when we need it, why do we have to wait for Him to speak with clarity or why won't He just say what He wants us to do without a lot of drama. She didn't say this with any disrespect or anything like that because I know this woman loves the Lord and the question she was asking if truth be told, some of us have asked those same questions, "Lord why can't you just give me the answers or directions now", I know I'm right about it. Well my answer to her was quite simple. *God is Sovereign and He's Head Honcho, in other words He calls the shots. Amen*

THE UNEXPECTED TEST

After leaving the hospital and lying around recuperating for a while, I was back on the battlefield doing what the Lord allowed me to do and what I realized I really missed. There was test where my children were concerned as we know that the enemy will come in any where he finds a opening. My daughter was an adult so there was not really much I went through with her, my son was another story, being a young man, now this is the main prey of Satan, a young black man. He was really having problems in school, first of all he loved to play football and for no reason that was visible to me, the coach wouldn't allow him playing time, now you probably say, I'm just being a mother and seeing no fault in her son, I promise you this was not the case, so he began to really rebel, and also I had made a bad move when he was in elementary school, out of my ignorance I had allowed them to place him in category of having a learning disability and for this reason he was put in a class that he didn't belong in, and I understood somewhat of what he was going through, be careful what you're told by educators concerning your children, get more information and different opinions, because it can affect the rest of their lives, well he began to cut school and I whipped him and punished and fussed and bribed and whatever I could think of to get him to go to school and one day he just told me; mama, you can whip me all you want but school just not for me, the children pass by the classroom and pick and laugh and I just don't want to go to school and unless it comes from me and I make up my mind to go it won't matter what you do to me. Well let me tell you the smoke began to come out my ears, but then I thought, maybe he's right because I can go on chasing and going through all this but he made a good point so I had to figure out what to do next because I didn't want him to be in a defeated mindset. So at the age of sixteen I allowed him to leave high school. After the decision to leave school had been reached, I searched for other options, and came up with the idea to send him away to Job Corps that way he would get a skill, so off to Kentucky he went. Now that episode in my life was taken care of and life sort of settled down. Well Satan was saying; so you think. I've learned in this life to never let my guard down, don't get too comfortable, you see Satan is on his job 24/7 (every day of the week, all day), we as saints of the Most High God, have to stay as faithful to the assignment that the Lord has given us. The next test and attack to place in my home in the form of the big "D" word, divorce. Going along thinking everything was fine at the beginning, we were working together in the prison ministry and going up and down the highway together, going to church together as a family, he was the chairman of the deacon board, and very dedicated around the church and to the pastor, the church referred to him as another **Stephen.** This was and still is a wonderful man that was just not strong enough to resist the fiery darts of the enemy, and he fell for the tricks of the enemy and it cost us our marriage, this was a man that was hard working, didn't stay out at night, a good provider for his family and if there was anything he even thought I wanted, he would get it for me, I never had to work unless I chose to do so, and he was always good to my children and for those reasons we have remained friends over the years. We can't look down on a person or persons that my have fallen by the wayside, for but for the Grace of God go ourselves, I continue to pray for him because God said that He is married to the backslider. After the divorce I had to really learn to trust and depend on God for my way of life had changed, not that I didn't have to depend on Him always but there was always a way made through my husband's paycheck, which I always had total control over, now some of you may be saying that I was my biggest problem, well let me clear that up, I asked him if there was something that needed to change in the marriage, because he also didn't want me to do any house work, even though he kept a full time job, and his answer to me was; if it's not broke don't fix it, so I assumed everything was ok. Again God taught me how to depend on Him, and He also began to give me a new mind set. I'm a person that regardless of what my trust has always been in God so it really wasn't hard for me to look to Him for my full support. Really things began to change in such a way, and as we go into the next chapter you'll see just how much and in what way, so don't stop reading. Let me get back to how subtle the devil is, first my husband started to work later and later, and then he started going less and less to the prison, and I asked him about this and he said that it just wasn't for him, well I could except that, then he started missing church, all of this gradually began to take place and before long, to divorce court we went, so the devil is very subtle, right? This was just a form of distraction, and distractions will take our focus off the things that the Lord has planned for us, follow this scene; you're sitting having a conversation with this person and you being very attentive to what is being discussed, well a bird flies down and lands on a spot right beside the person, well didn't that take your focus for a moment? That's the way the devil is, he will do anything in his power to take your mind off of the path that God has set before you.

ANOTHER DISTRACTION OR TWO

The night before I was to go and sign my final divorce decree I dropped a small section of butcher block table on my foot and busted my toe, I had to call my son and godson and they brought a couple of friends over(I guess I could be sort of dramatic at times, but I really busted my big toe) so I just stayed there in the chair that I had managed to reach and waited for them to arrive, when they got there they carried me to my bed and then they left. I had my cousin to come and drive me to the courthouse the next morning, with a sock on my foot and a cane in my hand and I went and took care of my business. The next day Jasmine and I were to be catching a flight to Ft. Lauderdale Florida, for a service that she was to be appearing at. That night I talked to God and this is what the conversation was all about, I said Father; I've got to go to the airport in the morning and I really don't want to have to go with a sock on my foot and carrying a cane, sometime during the night I got up and while walking through the hall in my home I realized that I was no longer limping, I tell you God had answered my prayer and I could go to the airport without the sock and the cane. Now the busted toe was distraction #1. While preparing to leave for the airport the next morning the phone rang and I answered it and it was my doctor, let me bring you up to speed, a couple of week prior to this time, I had be having some complications in my body and this same faithful cousin (this cousin is the daughter of my dearest cousin Beverly that was mentioned in Stepping Out, who has recently went on to be with the Lord) had taken me to my doctor and there were some test ran, so this call was the results of the test, distraction #2, the words the doctor spoke were; Mrs. King, we've gotten your test results back and it appears that you

40

have colon cancer, I told her these exact words; "thank you for calling, and you have a blessed day". In between removing the receiver from my ear and it reaching the cradle, I told the devil, Satan I'll not receive that from you and I rested the phone. (Cell phones were not the thing then). I continue to go about my business and we caught our flight. After this I began to call on people that I knew would know how to pray; Father heal Theresa, not Father if it be your will heal Theresa. I knew it was the Will of the Father that I am healed in Jesus Name; *Isaiah53:5 For he was wounded for our transgressions, he was bruised for our iniquities the chastisement of our peace was upon him; and with his stripes we are healed. 3John2:2 Beloved; I wish above all things that thou mayest prosper and be in health, even as thy soul prospereth.* While I'm away the saints are praying and interceding on my behalf, and we're trusting, believing and thanking God for my healing. When we got back home I had an appointment to see a specialist, well the prayers of the saints were yet going on and I had asked God to let the host of heaven surround me as I went in to see the specialist because I knew this would be an exploratory exam to determine how they were to treat the condition, well when I got there and before they prepared me for the exam I asked to go to the restroom and while in there I prayed and the Holy Ghost spoke to me and said; It's gone, it was there but its gone that God may be glorified. So I went back out and as the exam was getting under way I began to talk to the doctor and the nurse that was assisting him and I found out that they were also saints of the Most High God, because **we** praised Him as the drug began to take effect, this wasn't a sedative that would put me all the way out of it, I still was semi-conscious, and I heard the nurse tell the doctor; she has a good report to take back to her church, so praise God for the victory. I left the doctor's office from what they thought would be for them to find a way to treat colon cancer, but guess what "Doctor Jesus" had already been there. As we continue on there will other instances where I've found the Lord to be a doctor for me and mine. When I was told that I had this disease I immediately told God I wanted to be healed and didn't want to have to go in the hospital. About four years before this I had three aunts to pass away from cancer and it was hard on the family to see them like this and I asked God to please heal me because I didn't want my children to go through seeing me in that state, and God did just what I asked Him to do.

The Lord has said in His Word, be anxious for nothing but with prayer and supplication with thanksgiving, to let my request be made known unto God. I tell people all the time that I'm just crazy enough to believe every word in the bible is true, how about you?

New Adventures

Life is going on at a steady pace, we're now moving in a couple of different directions. Jasmine has been attending public school and as great and accommodating as the teachers and students tried to be this was not good educationally for Jasmine, she had a wonderful Braille teacher as well as a mobility instructor but there was no professionals for the other subjects that she needed, even though she needed the same subjects as the other students, there was a different way to teach her and they were just not equipped to do the task. So now there was a decision to be made. An agreed upon meeting was called to discuss the prospect of Jasmine attending an academy for the blind in another city, well I set at the meeting for as long as I could and when I couldn't control the tears any longer I called the meeting to a close, I couldn't stand the thought of letting her leave home, this was my baby. They had taken Jasmine outside of the meeting and after the meeting I went to get her and no one could tell me where she was and panic set in and children were running around every where and I almost lost it, but the Lord sent me right to where she was so patiently sitting. I got her and we went home, this was the end of her first week in middle school. While we were riding she and I talked about the academy and she knew I was upset, (Jasmine can always horn in on my emotions) she told me; mama don't worry, I'll be alright, to this day I still can hear that small voice of wisdom and understanding, she helped me to make the decision that needed to be made, she helped me to understand that she needed to be around her peers because in the elementary school that she attended she was the only one in the school that was totally blind and therefore she had to be signaled out for the paraprofessionals to work with and she really didn't like that. Finally I spoke with the people that I needed to speak with and agreed to allow Jasmine to attend the academy, but and there was a "but". When Jasmine started to attend the academy, I rented an apartment in the same city, even though I was purchasing my home here. Let me tell you about the goodness of the Lord, I did not have a job, but yet I moved into an apartment in that city and continued to pay my mortgage on my home also the same bills I had in Atlanta, I also had there instead of mortgage it was rent. Through the week we lived in Macon, Ga., and on the weekends we would get in the car and drive home until the following Monday, I thank God because He understood my heart and had compassion on me because I couldn't just let her go like that. We were at the school for about five months and then we got a call from Universoul Circus, and they wanted Jasmine to go on tour with them, they had met with us the previous year at a musical celebration where Jasmine was performing and we exchanged business cards. We decided to accept the offer and she was withdrawn from school. They arranged for us to fly out to Miami Florida and join the tour. This was the beginning of our first "living out of suitcases". Traveling with the circus was quit an experience, from watching movies over the years and observing circus living I found that Hollywood was on the money as to the day to day activities, walking through the trailer on the different lots and watching the different acts practicing and swinging from high wires and the animals in cages, all of the costumes, we had the option of staying in a trailer or a hotel in the different cities and states that we visited, but we opted to stay at the hotels, couldn't get with the porter potties. The circus built a scene for Jasmine, it was called the church scene, she closed every show with song and it was such a moving performance, the whole scene was so moving. We met a lot of people that we had only known of from television and radio. When I think back on these times, I'm overwhelmed with the many doors and opportunities that the Lord allowed and permitted in our lives. One of the performers had to leave the circus for some personal reason and I was given the opportunity to take that position, ok, this is the part I played, imagine me a circus performer. There is a song by Kirk Franklin, that talks about a mother praying for her dying son who has aids and so there I was kneeling beside the bed of this small boy with my hands folded in prayer and looking up toward heaven, I'm playing my part with all in me. I never would have thought I would be a part of the circus life. There was another role that I had while with the circus and this was not a pretend part, I was the chaplain for the circus and again here I was in the center of the ring, this time I was ministering the Word of God to people of different cultures, languages, and backgrounds, some didn't speak English, but you know what they attended anyway, this opened my spirit to understand that the Spirit of God is indeed universal, they got into the mist of the service as if I was speaking, Russian or Spanish or whatever their native language was, this let me see that we can receive from the Spirit in any setting where the true Word of God is being taught and preached, through faith they received the preached Word and by faith I was preaching before those that didn't speak the language, but this was only the Word of God being fulfilled. *Rom.10:14-15How then shall they call on Him in whom they have not believed? And how shall they hear without a preacher? And how shall they preach, except they be sent? As it is written, how beautiful are the feet of them that preach the gospel of peace, and bring glad tidings of good things.* I truly thank the Lord for these experiences that He allowed us during this time in our lives, I used to watch circus movies on TV, the flying acrobats and high wire walkers, along with the lion tamers and the small people and ring announces and again never in a million years would have even imagined this would one day be a part of my life. As you continue this walk with me you will experience more of the miraculous things that God allowed in my life and through these experiences my prayer is that your faith will reach a new level in *He who is able.* We continued to travel with the circus to many different cities and states and continued to meet many more prominent people. There was an opportunity for Jasmine to perform at a banquet for President Nelson Mandela from South Africa; we were able to meet members of his family and form friendships that to this day are still a part of our lives. This banquet took place in Brooklyn New York, we stayed in New York for six weeks and now that was a true experience, there was this street called Flatbush, and I would walk down this street and I promise you there were so many people on this street you could hardly see the pavement beneath your feet, this was one of the busiest places I've ever been to. I promise you I saw an emergency vehicle almost drive on the sidewalk because people didn't stop or pull over for emergency vehicles and it seemed that no one drove within the lanes if there were even lanes. There was always something going on in New York, the parks were full of activities with the musicians, dancers, vendors and the different dialects, visiting the different shops and buying designer clothes from New York, and I even went and had my ears pierced but the holes never healed so I ended up letting them close. Jasmine and I had such wonderful experiences. I don't tell you these things in a boastful way, but only to share with you how the Lord does those things that we feel unworthy of and would not believe could happen to us, but let me clear something up for you, I hear a lot of people say, and I used to say it myself; *"I'm not worthy of the things that God does for me"* no, not in ourselves we are not worthy, but because we have made Jesus Christ the Lord of our lives and because of His Redemptive Blood, we are now the Righteousness of God and therefore we are worthy through Him. Now stop calling yourself unworthy if the above statement fits you. Right before we left the circus, there was to be a trip to South Africa, now this story is going to blow some of your minds but before its all said and done I'll explain it to you ok. Now moving on, the trip was planned for some of the members of the group to travel to South Africa to perform and we were selected to be a part of those going, wow was I excited yet apprehensive. Well as excited as I was and Jasmine never seemed to get excited, as a matter of fact she never expressed a desire to go, just the opposite. From the beginning there was a problem with getting our shots and there were to be quite a few, and we couldn't seem to make it happen and then I decided to fly home so that we could get them in time and I couldn't get a flight that would allow us to get home and back in time for the next scheduled show, well the owner was going to work on that, then I stated to get these terrible headaches, like I hadn't experienced since becoming a born again Christian, I had suffered from migraine headaches before I accepted Christ in my life and once I did, I had been delivered from the migraines, well they seem to have started back. I noticed that when something would come up to make it seem as if we wouldn't be going on the trip and I would tell the right people, then the headaches would stop immediately,(true story) and as soon as I would allow myself to be persuaded to go and I would again accept, then the headaches would once again appear. Well I received the tickets and so Jasmine and I returned home to spend a few days before flying back to the circus and getting ready for the trip. The arrangements had been made for us to receive our shots when we got back to the circus, but one night while lying in bed with my head about to fall off my shoulders it was hurting so bad, I heard the voice of the Lord; He was instructing me to call and let the proper people know that we wouldn't be going on the trip, I began to explain to the Lord that I already had the tickets and plus it was about 2:00am, (as if He didn't already know these things) He went on to ignore what I had to say and told me to leave a voice message, well I did that and immediately my headache went away, and that was the last time we were with the circus, not because there was so called bad blood, but because the season would end once they got back and we just never renewed a contract. People asked me why I would pass up such an awesome opportunity and some even said I was crazy because I would probably never get another chance like that. I responses were like this," first of all God said we couldn't go" and "had we gotten on that plan, it's a possibility the thing would have fallen out of the sky", I don't know why God said no, but without a shadow of doubt I truly believe He did, and those headaches has never returned, yes I've had headaches since then but never to that magnitude. It's just a good thing to listen and obey the voice of God, regardless of how good something may look or seem to us, and the bible says in, *Prov.3:5-6 Trust in the Lord with all thine heart, and lean not unto thine own understanding. In all thy ways acknowledge Him, and He shall direct thy paths.*

WHO'S REPORT WILL YOU BELIEVE

Now that we're back home and Jasmine is getting ready to return to the academy, and yes I wanted to move back to that city while she was there, but the Lord let me know that either I trusted Him or I didn't, He said that He had allowed me to live there at the beginning and now it was time to allow her to become the person that He had called her to be and not only her, but that there were some things in me that also needed some work. I enrolled Jasmine in school and I stayed home in Atlanta. Now I didn't give up without a fight, (I imagine God was just shaking His head). This is what happened; I got in contact with the transportation system for the board of education, and where they were setting up a schedule for her to be picked up I asked for the job of driving her there at the beginning of the week and picking her up for the trip home at the end of the week, like I fore stated I'm sure the Lord was just looking down on me shaking His head and probably smiling, but He allowed favor to intercede and even though it was unprecedented, thy gave me the duties with pay, don't tell me what God won't do. *1Cor.1:27 But God has chosen the foolish things of the world to confound the wise; and God hath chosen the weak thing of the world to confound the things which are mighty.* See, in the natural that was a foolish thing for them to give me a job that the system already had in place that was to be operated by the guidelines of the system and not to create a position for me, who didn't even work within the system. When things like this happens, such as positions being created for you and doors open that you never imagined existed then you know that God is pulling some strings. So many things have happened in my life that I really can't tell it all, *clique right*? I find that to be so true, because while writing this book, there is so much that the Lord has done in my life; for me and to me that I really can't began to tell it all. When I think back on some of the foolish choices that I made while in my mess and then I think of what the consequences could have been, all I can do is really lift my eyes unto the hills, and give God all the Glory and Praise, because I know that it was only His great love for me and His purpose for my life. I realize that we were put here for God's purpose and regardless of what direction our lives may take, if the Lord has a divine plan for our lives then I truly believe that it will take place, now some may argue that with me but there will always be a difference in how we perceive some things. I think back on all the crooks and turns that I've made in my life and all the wasted time when I could have been doing something that would have brought about a different and maybe better more prosperous outcome, I've often asked myself this, and I think had that been the case then I wouldn't have had the testimony that has seemingly helped so many, and for that I give God all the Glory for it belongs to Him. I remember telling my dad once, when I talked to him about how my life at home had been (growing up) and how through it all, it had helped to mold me into the person that I've become with the inner strengths that I have over the years had to rely upon. I've learned that we all will have ***our hard pills to swallow*** as my grandmother used to say. There have been times when the enemy will come in an attempt to tear down my self-esteem, and self confidence, among other areas of my character as sure he has done to us all at one time or another, but that's what he does.

KEEPING UP THE PACE

Now that Jasmine is back at the academy and I'm back home and no longer driving her back and forth to Macon, GA. for school even though she's still there, this is another year and my job to transport has ended. I'm working now for Fulton County Board of Education and the location that I'm assigned to is in Fairburn, GA and that is 19 miles from home, this becomes a 38 mile round trip (follow me I'm going somewhere with this). Jasmine is leaving home every monday morning at 6:00am for school, in order to make her first class, her school is 83 miles from home and her is returned home every friday around 5:30pm. The favor of God worked in this in the sense that any residential student that was transported by city school buses had to be on campus on sunday evening, but by request and explaining that with our ministries, Jasmine was busy most sundays and couldn't return on sunday evenings and God showed His favor upon us once again. Now I'll tell you why I mentioned the distance that I travelled to work and back. I worked from 2:00pm until 11:00 so when Jasmine comes in on Friday evening I have to leave work and drive the 19 miles to meet the school bus and get Jasmine situated at home alone and then drive the 19 miles back to work and then drive the 19 miles back home again at 11:00, getting there between 11:30 and midnight. Now the Favor of God was constantly with me through all of this because my supervisor never reprimanded me for the 2+ hours it took for me to handle my situation every friday and I never got a speeding ticket even though I had to put the peddle to the metal sometimes in my going back and forth. Everything is going well at this time even though it's tiring me out and the fact that I had to leave Jasmine home alone every friday and how something may happen between the time I left work, a traffic jam, accident, car trouble or anything that would detain my making it home on time, or I was worried about what could happen with her, don't get me wrong I had faith and trust in God through all of this, but we know that test and trials do happen to God's people as well as others.

Following God's Lead

After being persistent in seeking the Lord on what to do about my predicament, He began to lead me in what to do. While at work one day (I was a custodian) pushing a dust mop down the hall I heard the voice of the Lord say: **Use what's in your hand**, now I can only imagine that my response was probably similar to what his was, when the Lord spoke to him and told him to use what was in his hand *Exodus 13:13 – 16 And Moses said unto the people, Fear ye not, stand still and see the salvation of the Lord, which he will show to you today: for the Egyptians whom ye have seen today ye shall see them again no more forever.*

14. The Lord shall fight for you and ye shall hold your peace.

15. And the Lord said unto Moses, Wherefore criest thou unto me? Speak unto the children of Israel that they go forward:

16. But lift thou up the rod and stretch out thine hand over the sea and divide it: and the children of Israel shall go on dry ground through the midst of the sea.

The following days the Holy Spirit continued to lead me because I found myself at work during my breaks making flyers for a cleaning service and going out to a new subdivision that had recently been built and sticking the flyers on mail boxes, but nothing seemed to happen and then one day I found myself going on the internet and finding a website that I had heard of that printed business cards that you could design yourself that was very inexpensive so I designed my cards and while doing this the Lord gave me the business name Tidy Up Cleaning Service, LLC. During this time I was so driven and I still had no idea what I was doing or how all this was going to come together but I did realize by now that God had a plan to make a way of escape for me out of my situation. I continued to go out and not only pass out flyers but now I also had cards with my name and the a business name, all of this was sort of surreal also as if I'm totally outside of what is going on around me and I'm just watching everything take place. I remember seeing this episode on the "Twilight Zone" where this couple was lost in this town and everything they touched turned out to be a prop and that couldn't escape the town and couldn't understand why, well at the end of the picture it turned out that there was a little girl playing with her doll house and this couple was the actual dolls and she had control of their fate. So this is the way I felt, and I thank God that He was the one in control of my every movement. Now follow me with this, I'm still trying to get some work for the company during this time and still working for the Board of Education. One day during my lunch break I went into the sub-division and there was a guy working on a new home and I approached him and asked if he was in charge of the building and he said that he was and I asked if he needed a cleaning crew and he informed me that the owner of the company in charge of building the home had a crew that he had been using for a long time and as far as he knew, the man was happy with them, as I walked back to my vehicle I remember saying to God; You told me I could have this business and it's mine. Well I went back to work and continued to go about my routine. That next week there was a notice posted at the school about positions in Administrations available and being tired of what I was doing and wanting a change I made an appointment to go and take the exam, well I fell short of the WPM (words per minute) so that fell through, the test was held before work at another location and therefore you would have time to report to work but I decided not to go and said to myself that I would just go home and that's what I did, went home and lay down across my bed and I hadn't been long before the phone rang, I answered it and it was the builder that I had spoken to a week or so ago and he informed me that the owner of the company was looking for a new janitorial crew because he was no longer pleased with the one that he had (WOW, Look at God) and if I could get there in an hour he wanted to meet with me, well now what do you think I did?, RIGHT!! I jumped up from that bed and made my way to meet with this man and when I met him he looked just like Kenny Rogers and I introduced myself and he did the same and he asked me how long had I been in the business and I answered like this; I'm just now starting my business but I've cleaned for the Board of Education off and on for the last 20 years of so and I've had to run and clean my own home behind children and sometime pets, but if you give me a chance you won't regret it. Well this was in 2005, and Tidy Up Cleaning Service LLC., is still up and running 20016. The name of the company was Custom Builders and they among others were clients of mine for several years until the recession came along. Now after I secured a contract with them I still kept my job, but after about a month The Lord spoke and told me to retire from my job, He's still leading my destiny at this time and so I began to tell my co- workers that I was close to that I was going to retire and they would ask me why they couldn't understand because had good benefits and the pay was good and had it not been for the Lord I'm sure I wouldn't have understood that move by someone else. Well one day the Lord spoke and said *do it now,* it just so happened that I was sitting in the library with my co-worker when He spoke and I told her I'm going to do it now and she said why and I told her because the Lord just told me to, well as I walked out of the library thinking that I would have to go and fine my supervisor, there he was coming down the hall in my direction and I asked him if I could speak to him for a moment and he said sure and so I told him that I wanted to turn in my resignation and he had the same **"why"** as everyone else and I had the same speech ready for him, so he told me that I would have to fill out the paperwork and turn it in to the principal and when I went to turn in the paperwork to the principal, **(you got it, he had the same "why" and I had the same speech ready for him).** I didn't understand a lot of what was taking place nor the logic in it all, remember I was resigning from a pretty good paycheck, which was the only one coming into my home at the time and I'm not the only one that I'm responsible for, so what I really learned was the meaning of was a couple of scriptures among many that I began to trust in.

Psalm 37:3 - 4 Trust in the Lord, and do good; so shalt thou dwell in the land, and verily thou shalt be fed.

4. Delight thyself also in the Lord; and he shall give thee the desires of thine heart.

Then there was King David who said in Psalm 37:25, 26

25 I have been young, and now am old' yet have I not seen the righteous forsaken, nor his seed begging bread.

26 He is ever merciful, and lendeth; and his seed is blessed.

I left the job and believe it or not two other co-workers resigned also, not the same day but not long after and both went on to something better, because of the faith that I walked in and the God that I talked about and trusted in, it helped to build their faith. God is so good, if we just remember His Word and allow Him to lead us not only when we are facing challenges but in our daily walk. *Remember Proverbs 3:5, 6*

5 Trust in the Lord with all thine heart; and lean not unto thine own understanding.

6 In all thy ways acknowledge him, and he shall direct thy path.

Walking In The Overflow

The business is "Booming" I have contracts coming from everywhere and I'm able to employ a full crew during this time. I'm operating in a way that I never dreamed could be possible. Tidy Up Cleaning Service is on the map, I'm working with some of the top builders and building contractors in the state of Georgia as well as other states in the near south, I'm registered with the Federal, State, County, and City Procurement Offices. Jasmine is away at school during the week so I'm able to work freely and be assured that she's ok. (Remember, earlier I mentioned that the Lord spoke and told me He would take care of her). I tell you, that all of this that is going on is blowing my mind. *1Cor. 2:9 But as it is written, EYE HATH NOT SEEN, NOR EAR HEARD, NEITHER HAVE ENTERED INTO THE HEART OF MAN, THE THINGS WHICH GOD HATH PREPARED FOR THEM THAT LOVE HIM.* That scripture truly fit the place in my life at the time. I was contracted to do school, newly constructed homes, newly built hotels and newly built sub-divisions among a few projects; again, never in my wildest dreams did I even envision this in my life. I truly believe that the lord has seasons for our lives and blessings and I was in my season with the business at this time. *Eccl. 3:1 To every thing there is a season, and a time to every purpose under the heaven. John 16:24 Hitherto have ye asked nothing in my name: ask, and ye shall receive, that your joy may be full.* My joy was totally complete, I often thought back to when I had first began to talk to the Lord about my situation with working and having to be there for Jasmine also, which was my first priority, then and still is to this day and how He had made a way for us that was far above anything I could imagine. *John 10:10 The thief cometh not,*

but for to steal and to kill, and to destroy: I am come that they might have life, and that thy might have it more abundantly. The business began to receive calls from other states as well local, for the first several it was really booming and I'm putting more people to work that operate in different areas of the janitorial service, window cleaners, and floor techs. During this time the business was blessed with two heavy duty pieces of floor equipment and they were given freely to me, this equipment ran into the thousands of dollars. God is really showing His Mighty Hand at work in my life, but even in all of this my prayer has always been that He would keep me clothed in Humility. All is running smoothly and then the drop in the economy comes with a bang and it brings with it a domino effect in the housing business;

    a.   No one is buying lots in which to build on
    b.   No one is building
    c.   There is no work for the painters
    d.   There is no work for janitorial
    e.   There is no work for landscapers

And so forth and so on. Well the booming season for that part of my life had slowed down tremendously but the business was still moving but at a much slower pace, many contractors closed their doors but the Lord kept our doors open. Praise Him.

HE LAID HIS HANDS ON ME

As we know in this life there will be physical sickness and diseases, as well as mental, and emotional but in all of this there is a Healer among us, The Man Jesus. Let me share a few instances in my life where I found out for myself of His healing powers and like the centurion, He didn't have to come to my house to heal me all He had to do was send forth the healing virtues from heaven. There was a time when I was having issues in my body and went to the doctor to find out what was going on and there were test ran and I went home and as Jasmine and I were getting ready one morning about two weeks later the phone rang and this was a phone that was set in a cradle (some of you may not remember this) as I answered it on the other end was my doctor and her words were; I have received your test results and it appears that you have colon cancer, well I told her thank you for the call and between removing the phone from my ear and placing it back in the cradle, I told the devil; I'll not receive that from you. There was a lot going on at this time, this was the third morning after I dropped the table top on my foot and busted my toe and had to wear a sock, and the day after going downtown and filing for divorce with a sock on my foot and a cane in my hand, hobbling all the way, but praise God I was able to put a shoe on at this time because I had prayed not to have to go to the airport with a sock on and certainly not to appear in the state of the event where Jasmine was to perform. We few out the next morning as scheduled, when I got back home I called on some of the saints of God that I knew would pray for me and with me, I called on the saints that would pray, knowing and believing that it was God's will that I be healed and not the ones that would pray; Lord if it be your will, heal her, even though they would have meant well. Life goes on and we were praying and trusting God for a good report. During this time I had a sister in Christ that is a Prophetess which was also praying for me, when I called her and asked her to stand in agreement with me for my healing and began to tell her what was going on she began to tell me of a vision that she had concerning me and now she knew why and this is the vision she had and these are her words; I had a vision of being inside your stomach and I was scraping and scraping with my hands and I was crying and I didn't understand why I was having this open vision, and now I know why. We prayed together and then I went about my day with her letting me know that she would continue to be in prayer. One Sunday during church service there was a speaker there from Nigeria that the pastor when he introduced him was someone that he met walking down the street and they began to talk and while the talking, the Lord lead him to invite the gentlemen to be a speaker, during the service the speaker called a prayer line and when I walked up he told my pastor's wife to place her hand on me, (COGIC, men don't place their hands on a woman's body, at least not back then) and he told me to raise my hands (keep in mind no one except my husband knew what was going on with me and he had not spoken to anyone) and this is what he said: woman of God the Lord says no more cancer in your body and that you will have more wealth in your life than you've ever dreamed of, Praise God, did the tears began to flow because I knew that I had heard from the Lord. Three weeks later I had to go to the cancer specialist that my doctor had setup for me to see, when I got there and the nurse began to get me ready for prep, the doctor came in and I asked if could go to the restroom before getting on the gurney and the doctor said sure, when I got in the restroom, "Praise God" The Holy Ghost spoke, and this is what He said; It's gone, make no mistake about it, it was there but now it's gone. I feel He spoke this to me so I'd know without a doubt that the cancer had been there and on one could say they read the test/x-rays wrong. Well I made my way back to the room where the doctor and his nurse was waiting for me and got on the gurney. During the time I was waiting for this appointment, a portion of my prayer was that the lord would send the host of heaven to surround me. Praise be to God, before they put me under a light anesthesia the doctor, nurse and myself were praising God and Thanking Him. While I was under I heard the nurse say to the doctor; she's got a good report to take back to her church, God is to be and is and was praised. I never had to see that doctor again and never heard from him again. Here's another praise report, I had to go in for my annual mammogram and a couple of weeks later I received a letter from the hospital stating that there were some masses found in my breast and I needed to come in for more test, (mind you I wasn't concerned because I remembered and believed what God had said through His servant that Sunday in church) so I made an appointment and went back for the test. I got to the hospital and was brought into the exam room and had the x-rays taken, after the x-rays were finished the nurse asked me to have a seat in the waiting area and to not get dressed until the doctor read the x-rays, well after the doctor read the x-rays I was asked to return back to the exam room for more x-rays, once getting back inside and she getting the instruments set back up, I asked her if she would turn the monitor so that I could see as she shot the x-rays and what I saw was masses in both breast, and so she shot one x-ray and the masses were still there and then she shot another and they were still and then she shot the third one and ***Praise God Everything Cleared Up!!!*** Now I'm going to share one more praise report, even though I could go on and on like the Energizer Bunny that goes on and on or the Timex, that takes a licking and keeps on ticking. I had been experiencing an issue in my stomach and so I went to the hospital once again and when I got there the doctors wanted to and did put a tube down my throat and it traumatized my body and it was so painful and uncomfortable, and then one of their phones rang and as soon as he got off of the phone he spoke with some urgency and told them to take the tube out of my throat. They keep me that night because they said they would have to run another test that could only be done on Monday and this was a Saturday night. That night I was assigned a room and the next morning a nurse came in my room pushing a big machine and she informed me that they were there to do the test and I told her that I had been told that the test couldn't be done until Monday morning and she informed me that, that was the way it was normally done but the doctor wanted it done that morning (again God's favor, but keep reading, you haven't heard it all yet) she proceeded to introduce herself; my name is nurse Comfort, and then she spelled and then she went on to tell me that the doctor would be in shortly and that his name was Dr. Sunshine, wow, after hearing this I knew the Holy Spirit was there with me, the Lord let me know through the names of this people that He was truly with me, now when the doctor came in I began to tell him about the tube they had put down my throat and how it had hurt me and then he told me that he was the one that had called and when they informed him about the tube, he's the one that told them in no uncertain terms to take it out. Praise God for every time He has been there and is still here and will always be here. You probably think I'm sickly or have been but this is far from the truth, I'm pretty healthy, I think these situations came about so that the Lord could show me that He's an ever present help in the times of trouble. I'm so grateful that I know the Lord for myself and I don't have to go on anyone else's report.

When Man Said No Way, God Said His Way

I remember sometimes thinking down through the years how I wish I could have done some things differently, on being going on through school when I should have (that story is in "Stepping Out") so I often wished I could go on to college but I just didn't feel it would happen, I had been to school on several schools since becoming an adult but there was still and emptiness. I wanted to go to school to feel nearer to Christ is that makes any sense to anyone but me. I went and enrolled in a Bible College that was the school my dad attended, after being there a couple of semesters for my Bachelor's Degree, I realized I just wouldn't be able to afford it so I dropped out with a heavy heart, realizing this is what was missing and this is what I wanted to go to school for. Keep reading and I'm going to once again show you the **Favor of God.** One day I went to this church to drop off some information about Jasmine, and I met with the pastor and I had never been here before and after explaining my visit he told me he would look over everything and get back with me and we shook hands and I left his office and while out in his secretary's office preparing to leave, he stuck his head out of his office and asked me if I could come back in for a moment before I left and so before leaving I went back to his office and he offered me a seat and began to tell me that the Lord had spoken to him concerning me when I walked out of his office(God don't mess around, right?) everybody that know me know that I'm a weeper when it comes to the moving of the Spirit, my eyes began to well up at this time and he asked me what was it that I needed and I just began to bare my burdens and I didn't know that

I was carrying so much, and I'm letting the tears flow at this time and I'm kind of upset with myself because here I am crying in front of someone that I don't even know and on top of that I'm telling him my business and I can't seem to stop either one, then we began to talk about my wanting to be able to go to school and get my degree in Theology, but not being able to afford it, and "To God be the Glory", this pastor began to tell me that when the Lord spoke concerning me, He has told him to do everything he could for me, and then he went on to tell me that he was the President of a Christian University (I'm wiping the tears as I write this) he told me don't worry you'll get everything you desire. This man was true to his word and obedient to God instructions, I went to his University and not only did he allow me to study and achieve my Bachelor's Degree in Christian Counseling and my Master's Degree in Theology. God is so good man said because I didn't go the normal way through school this wouldn't be possible, I even told myself this during my moments of feeling defeated or weary, we get this way sometimes but thank God for Jesus. Many times the Holy Spirit has had to come and encourage me during these times and minister to me when no one else could or would. Now the Lord didn't stop here, I was talking to one of my sister's in Christ one day and it just came out, I told her, someone is going to give me a doctorate, and about a week later while talking to this man of God, he told me that he was nominating me to receive an Honorary Doctorate, you could have knocked me over with a feather, then he said, I'm the president and it has to go before the board but with my recommendation I'm sure you're get it, and guess what; today I'm Dr. Theresa Stokley, I don't share this to boast or brag on me but to brag on my God and His divine Favor in my life. What I've shared is just a tip or what the Lord has allowed in my life and moved out of my life. We are the righteousness of God through Christ Jesus and we can call those things that be not as though they were, according to the Word of God.

Happy Birthday

We've made a lot of memories, throughout our childhood days
no worries in this great big world, all we did were play

We always had each other's back, that I could count on you.
even now since we're all grown up, I know that still is true

I can't even remember, the first time I saw your face;
But I do know within my heart, no one can take your place.

They called me Ole' Soul, and called you Slim, I hope you're not
that old to remember, we were born the same year.

We're there for each other, and will be to the end.
By blood we are cousins, and by hearts we are friends

Pastor, Theresa Stokley

Happy Birthday

My sweet cousin, and a
HAPPY NEW YEAR!

In loving memory
Mrs. Beverly Adams-Crawford

I talked about this person in the first book, for those of you who didn't get to meet her through my writing about her then, let me tell you a little about her, she was my first cousin biologically but in reality she was so much more to me, she was a confidant, friend and as some would say when we were younger, my partner in crime. We were born the same year, she in July me in December so I called her "Big Cuz and she called me "Lil Cuz" and sometimes we would tease the other about who was the oldest as we got older. I officiated at her wedding, not even imagining that on December 19, 2015, I would be doing the eulogy for my friend, my cousin, my sister. I miss her so much, sometimes as I think about all the memories we shared and the conversations we shared I find myself still crying for her, there were things we did for each other that no one else even knew about and things we shared in conservations and the tears and laughter we shared with each other. I still can hear that funny laugh she had, she would get so tickled sometimes and then she could sing also, she had a beautiful voice. I remember when she was in the hospital and I prayed and asked God to please don't take this one, no God not this one, but God knows best and she was in so much pain. I'll always have a special place in my heart for my "Big Cuz". She was known by some as the Queen of Facebook, and she took all the pictures during family reunions and other occasions and just to take, she kept up with all the family history and someone asked during the repass, who's gonna take the pictures now? This is a birthday card that she made for me in 2014 and posted it on facebook (she was a poet also)and I didn't see it because I don't do much facebook, but while at my sister's house during the passing of my brother-n-law in 2015, she came to me and asked me if I saw my card that she had made for me and I told her no and she said, wait let me get my phone and pull it up, she came back and pulled it up and read it to me and my eyes got so watery and I gave her a hug, not realizing that less than a year later she would be leaving me, I'll forever cherish that birthday card. Love you Big Cuz, rest on in the Bosom of Jesus.

Some of my children from the past

I've spoken in both books about some of my "kids' from the old neighborhood where the old was and the new took over. These children were my children, to them I was Ms. Theresa, a lot of the parents would call me when the kids would get a little hard headed and didn't want to listen. They're grown now with children of their own. I've lost touch with some of them and sometimes like on my birthday or mother's day I'll get a greeting on facebook or a card and sometimes they will have talked to someone and gotten my phone number and given me a call, when I run into one of them in passing there is always a smile and a hug. I have fond memories of "my kids". One became doctor, city worker, truck driver, cosmologist, mothers, fathers, minister and just different walks of life, some have gone on to rest with the Lord, and for the ones I haven't seen or heard from, I keep them in my heart of hearts. I'm going to name a few:

Alexis J. Stokley- Preacher (my son)
Schgathan Carmichael
Yolanda Seabron – Fat (my daughter)
Qudeski Curtis - Deck
Joe Clark
Lexi Clark – Ninja
Kenya Walker
Lynn Walker
Marco Walker
Eddie Bell
Eyonis Redford
Misty Clark
Samone Ferguson – Monie
Delveccio
Stacy
Corey Lowe
Corinthian Zachery –Cousin James

These are just a few and if any of you read this book and don't see your name written please know that it's written on my heart.

Love you all and thanks for the memories, love and respect that you've given me over the years.

Printed in the United States
By Bookmasters